The King and the Sea

Heinz Janisch · Wolf Erlbruch

The King and the Sea

21 Extremely Short Stories

Heinz Janisch · Wolf Erlbruch

Translated by Sally-Ann Spencer

GECKO PRESS

The King and the Sea

"I am the king!" said the king.
The sea answered with a *whoosh*.
"Hmm." The king cocked his head thoughtfully.
"I see," he murmured.
And he stood there quietly, listening to the waves.

The King and the Cat

"What are you doing?" asked the king.
"Warming my coat in the sun," said the cat,
stretching out on the grass.
"The sun means a lot to you then," said the king.
"Yes," said the cat. "Today the sun is my king."

The king thought for a moment.
Then he took off his coat, lay down beside the cat,
and let the sun warm his skin.

The King and the Shadow

"Why do you have to follow me around?" asked the king.
"To stop you from coming up with stupid ideas," said the shadow.
"And to remind you there are two sides to every story."
"So there are," murmured the king, staring at the
long dark shadow cast by his small gold crown.

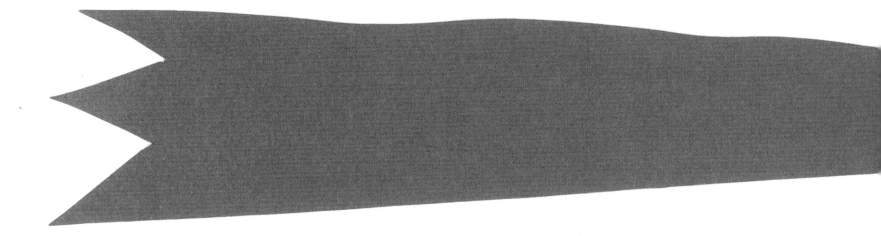

The King and the Rain

"My crown's going to get rusty," said the king. "Can't you stop?"
"Even if I do," said the rain, "your crown will still rust.
And so will you."

"True," said the king when he'd thought it over.
"In that case, I might as well take a shower."
So he stood outside with his face to the sky
and let the rain wash his cheeks.

The King and the Tree

"What do you do with your crown?" asked the king.
"Well," said the tree, "I let birds live in it. And the wind.
Children hide there, too."
"I see," said the king, and he stood for a while
listening to the leaves.

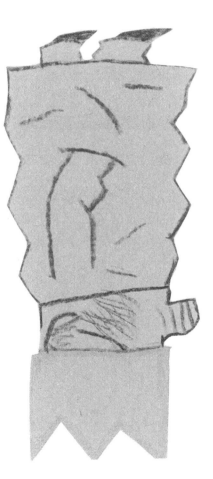

The King and the Squirrel

"I can do handstands," the king told the squirrel.
"And headstands."
The squirrel watched the king do a handstand,
then a headstand.
"I can stand on one leg," said the king.
"And walk backwards with my eyes closed."
The king showed the squirrel.
The squirrel watched without a word, then he
bounded to the top of the highest tree and
disappeared among the twigs and leaves.
The king stood and stared after him.
"I can run really fast as well," he called.

The King and the Dog

"Sit! Lie! Come!" shouted the king. "I am the king!"
"Stop! Fetch! Heel!" he bellowed.
Then he ran off after the dog.

The King and the Ghost

"I don't believe in ghosts," said the king.

"I don't believe in kings," said the ghost.

"Then one of us must be mistaken," said the king.

"So it seems," said the ghost, spiriting himself away.

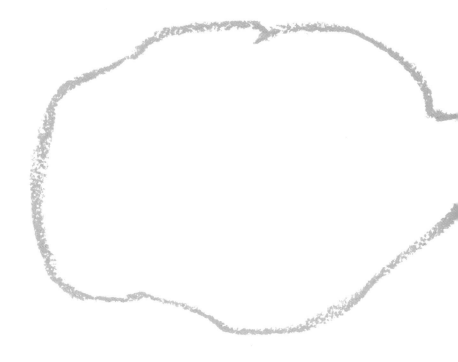

The King and the Cloud

"Hello up there!" said the king to the cloud.
"On your way so soon? Why don't you stay?
You won't find a nicer kingdom: green hills,
lush fields, loamy soil. There are towers as high as—"
But the cloud had already moved on.
"I see," said the king with a quiet sigh.

The King and the Trumpet

"I am the king," said the king. "Play for me!"
The trumpet kept quiet.
"I command you," said the king.
The trumpet said nothing.
The king held it to his lips and blew gently.
The trumpet made a faint *parp*.
"That's better," said the king.
He looked at the trumpet.
"I suppose you don't like playing on your own."
He waited for a moment.
"Oh, all right," he said, taking a deep breath.

The King and the Fishing Net

"Why are you full of holes?" the king asked the net. "How will you catch everything for me like that?"

"I won't catch everything," said the net. "Only a few fish. The sea has to stay where it is. That's why I have holes."

"That makes sense," said the king, clearing his throat. "What would I do with the sea at my palace? Who has room for a whole ocean?"

The King and the Bee

"Buzz off," said the king, shooing the bee from his flower.
"Don't you know I'm the king?"
"And I'm the queen," said the bee, stinging the king's nose.

The King and the Picture

"You're beautiful," the king said to the bird on his wall.

"Thank you. I think so, too," said the bird. "But I'm missing something."

"What's that?" asked the king.

"The wind under my wings," said the bird, flying away.

The King and Sleep

"I'm the one in charge here," said the king.
"I'll decide when I'm tired. I'm the king."
He yawned. "I know your tricks," he said, sitting up straighter.
"A king doesn't take orders from anyone."

He talked for a while, but his head was growing heavy
and his crown began to slip.
"Whoops," he muttered, catching it just in time.
Then he fell asleep.

The King and the Night

"I can't see a thing," the king said to the night. "How about
a bit more light?"
"You'll have to talk to the day," said the night. "I look after
darkness; the day takes care of light."
"I can do both," said the king, fetching a candle.

The King and the Star

"What are you good for?" asked the king. "You're so far away
I can't reach you. What am I supposed to do with you?"
The star disappeared.
"Hey, it's all dark! Come back!" The king stared up at the
black sky. "I miss you."
"You see?" said the star, and gave the king a dazzling wink.

The King and the Sky

"I need a blanket," said the king. "This minute!
And make it a good one."
With that, it began to snow.
Soft flakes fell around him.
"There's your blanket," said the sky as it covered the
landscape in glittering white.
The king gazed in wonder. "Thank you," he said.

The King and Salt

"My dinner tastes bland," cried the king.
"Someone forgot the salt."
He heard roaring as doors and windows flew open,
and the sea rushed in over the table.
"That's more like it," said the king, picking up his fork.

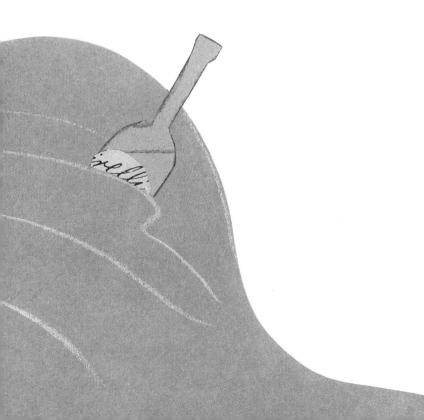

The King and the Pencil

"Talk to me," said the king to the pencil. "Say something!
Say YIKES or OUCH or THINGAMEBOB."
"Glad to oblige," said the pencil with a nod.

The King and the Book

"How are you?" enquired the king.

"That's what I've been asking you all along," said the book.

The King and the Kings

The king stood on the shore.
"Here we are: the sea, the sky, the sun, and me. Kings, all of us."
He swelled with pride.
Just then an enormous shadow loomed beneath the waves
and a mountain rose from the water.
The king was astonished. "A whale," he said.
A moment later, a small crab scuttled over his bare toes
and a white butterfly brushed against his nose.
"All right, all right," said the king. "You've made your point."
He took off his crown and placed it on the sand.
With a shout of laughter, he leaped into the sea.

Heinz Janisch is an Austrian children's book writer whose books have been published in more than a dozen languages and won many international awards.

Wolf Erlbruch is a celebrated German author and illustrator who won the 2006 Hans Christian Andersen Medal for Illustration. He wrote and illustrated *Duck, Death and the Tulip*, published in English by Gecko Press.

This edition first published in 2015 by Gecko Press
PO Box 9335, Marion Square, Wellington 6141, New Zealand
info@geckopress.com

First American edition published in 2015 by Gecko Press USA, an imprint of Gecko Press Ltd.
A catalog record for this book is available from the US Library of Congress.

Distributed in the United States and Canada by Lerner Publishing Group, www.lernerbooks.com
Distributed in the United Kingdom by Bounce Sales and Marketing, www.bouncemarketing.co.uk
Distributed in Australia by Scholastic Australia, www.scholastic.com.au
Distributed in New Zealand by Random House NZ, www.randomhouse.co.nz

A catalogue record for this book is available from the National Library of New Zealand.

Original title: *Der König und das Meer*
© Sanssouci im Carl Hanser Verlag München 2008

Written by Heinz Janisch · Illustrated by Wolf Erlbruch · Translated by Sally-Ann Spencer ·
Edited by Penelope Todd · Typesetting by Spencer Levine, New Zealand
Printed in China by Everbest Printing Co Ltd, an accredited ISO 14001 & FSC certified printer

ISBN hardback 978-1-877579-94-3
ISBN paperback 978-1-927271-80-3

For more curiously good books, visit www.geckopress.com